KEEP LOOKING!

by Millicent Selsam and Joyce Hunt
illustrated by Normand Chartier

Macmillan Publishing Company   New York
Collier Macmillan Publishers   London

This house looks empty. The yard looks empty.
Snow covers the ground. But there are animals here.
Where are they? Sit quietly, wait patiently,
and keep looking.

Here comes a chickadee. It is flying to the fat
hanging in an orange net in the lilac bush.

A blue jay hops on the same branch. It is going after
some seed in the bird feeder on the branch higher up.
It screeches and chases the chickadee away.

Now look down on the ground. Do you see
juncos, or snowbirds, pecking at the seeds
that the blue jay dropped?

A squirrel is stealing seed from the bird feeder.

Now a chipmunk pops up from its nest in the woodpile.
Did it hear the squirrel?

A family of bluebirds
lived in this birdhouse
all summer long.
They went south for the winter.
Who lives here now?
Look. A mouse moved in.

The rabbit is hiding in the raspberry bushes.
It is wiggling its nose. It smells something.
Can it smell a fox?
It thumps and hops back to its hole.

Look at the hole in the ground. It is the entrance
to the dark burrow of the woodchuck, fast asleep
under the ground. For the woodchuck it is nighttime
all winter long.

A heap of garter snakes are keeping one another warm
at the bottom of this pile of rocks. They also sleep
through the winter.

The box turtle is sleeping. It, too, has found a place underground where it can escape the winter cold. Cardinals and titmice feed on the ground above.

Ants have moved down from their nests in the ground
to even deeper passageways where they won't freeze.
They climb one on top of another to keep warm.

Behind the stairs leading to the house, there are old,
torn spiderwebs. When you look close you can see little
balls hanging on the threads. They are spider eggs.
They will become next year's spiders.

Near the torn spiderwebs is a cocoon.
Inside the cocoon something is happening.
A moth will hatch out in the spring.

It is nighttime—the moon is shining.
There is a loud noise.

The raccoons have found the garbage cans.

The owl is awake. It is calling. It sounds like
"Who cooks for you? Who cooks for you?"
The mouse in the birdhouse trembles.

Two skunks are taking a walk. The moonshine
lights up their white stripes.

Whoosh!
You can hear the soft flapping of wings.
Is it a bird? No, most birds do not fly at night.
It is a bat swooping out of the attic.

If you get up early one morning, just before the sun
rises, and sit patiently at the window, you may
see a deer nibbling on the twigs of the maple tree.

Here is the house again.
How many animals can you find?

Animals in This Book and the Pages Where They Appear

To the house in the country—M.S. and J.H.

To the gift of little eyes, especially Molly's and Sam's—N.C.

Text copyright © 1989 by Millicent Selsam and Joyce Hunt. Illustrations copyright © 1989 by Normand Chartier. All rights reserved. No part of this book may be reproduced or transmitted in any form or by any means, electronic or mechanical, including photocopying, recording, or by any information storage and retrieval system, without permission in writing from the Publisher. Macmillan Publishing Company, 866 Third Avenue, New York, NY 10022. Collier Macmillan Canada, Inc. Printed and bound in Japan. First American Edition   10 9 8 7 6 5 4 3 2 1   The text of this book is set in 14 point Trump Medieval. The illustrations are rendered in watercolor on rag paper.

Library of Congress Cataloging-in-Publication Data   Selsam, Millicent Ellis, date. Keep looking! / by Millicent Selsam and Joyce Hunt; illustrated by Normand Chartier.—1st American ed. p. cm.   Summary: As the reader turns the page, a new animal is added to an illustration of a country home in the winter. ISBN 0-02-781840-3 1. Wildlife watching—Juvenile literature. 2. Animals—Juvenile literature. [1. Wildlife watching. 2. Animals.] I. Hunt, Joyce. II. Chartier, Normand, date, ill. III. Title. QL60.S45 1988 599—dc19 88-1416 CIP AC

DATE DUE

2 A 1994

OCT 2 1994

NOV 2 1 1994

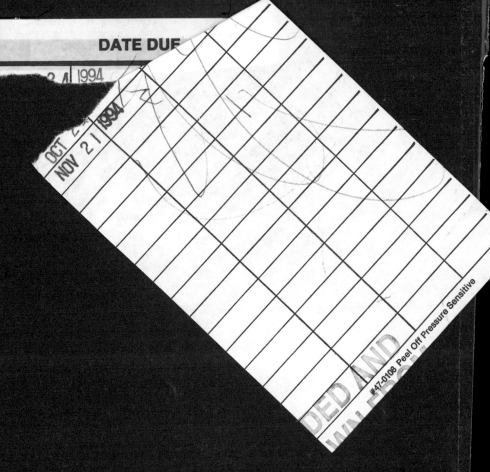

#47-0108 Peel Off Pressure Sensitive

DISCA
WITHDRA
WARWICK PUBLIC
LIBRARY